PENGUINAUT!

WRITTEN BY **Marcie Colleen**   ILLUSTRATED BY **Emma Yarlett**

ORCHARD BOOKS / NEW YORK

To Mom and Dad, for being
my launch pad. —Marcie

For Isaiah and Solomon,
—love Emma

Text copyright © 2018 by Marcie Colleen
Illustrations copyright © 2018 by Emma Yarlett

Library of Congress Cataloging-in-Publication Data Available

ISBN 978-0-545-84884-8

10 9 8 7 6 5 4 3 2   19 20 21 22 23

Printed in China   38
First edition, November 2018

The text type was set in Warnock Pro Bold.
The title type was hand-lettered by Emma Yarlett.
The illustrations were done in watercolor,
collage, pencil, crayon, pen, and paint.
Book art direction and design by Marijka Kostiw

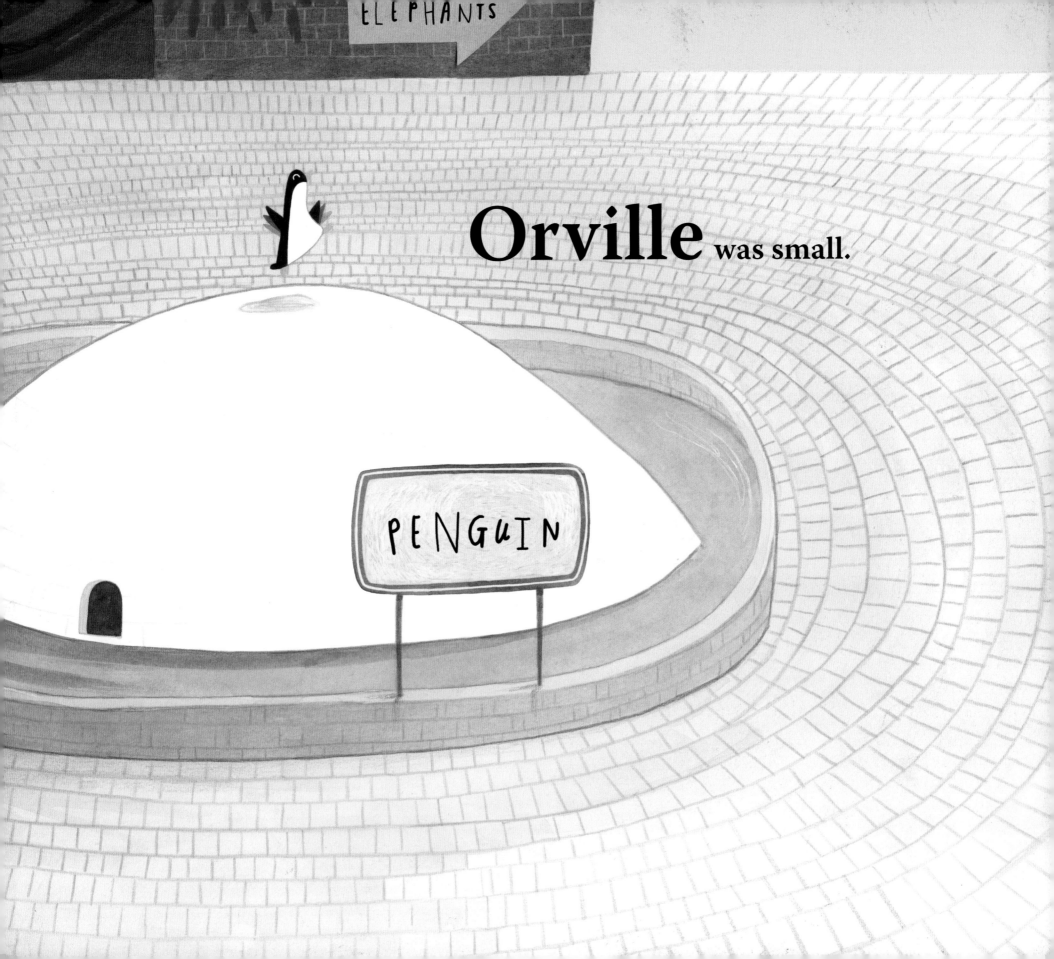

Orville was small.

His friends were BIG.

And their
adventures
were BIGGER.

Orville longed for *big* adventures, too.

One day, he announced his plans for the **biggest** and best adventure yet.

Orville flippered out.

He tried to flap — KERPLOP!

He tried to climb — WHACK!

He tried to catapult — fa-LING!

. . . and landed in the reptile house.
Orville was pretty sure the
boa constrictor was not trying to hug him.

Still Orville kept trying.

He borrowed from
the zookeeper.
He nicked from
the trash cans.
He built and built.

And with a **shake,** **shake,** **shake** of a half-filled soda bottle, the ship was ready for liftoff.

It was perfect.

And perfectly

penguin-sized.

With a trembling flipper salute,

he took his place at the controls.

BLAST-OFF!

WHOOSH!

The ship zipped through the night sky,

through clouds, over stars,

and straight to the moon.

Orville landed.

His stomach
felt queasy.
His spacesuit
felt squeezy.
Now that
he'd made it,
what would
he do?

He took a small step.

He hopped.

Did a little dance.

And tripped.

TUMBLE BUMBLE

He somersaulted with stars,

cartwheeled over craters,

BA

BOING!

and giggled for all the galaxy to hear.

It was the BIGGEST and best adventure yet.

"I'm doing it myself!" he cheered,

but his tiny voice was swallowed up

in the starry blackness.

Orville stopped.

He was all alone.

His stomach grew queasier.

His spacesuit grew squeezier.

He shivered

and a note fell out

of his pocket.

He missed his friends.

So Orville

closed his eyes

tightly

and imagined

they were

there.

When he was safely back in his ship,

he looked toward home.

He couldn't wait to tell everyone

about his **big** adventure.

Sure, Orville's friends
were BIG.
Now, the proud Penguinaut
felt BIG, too.

ELEPHANT'S

ORVILLE

ORVille

Being together
was out
of this world.

3, 2, 1 . . .

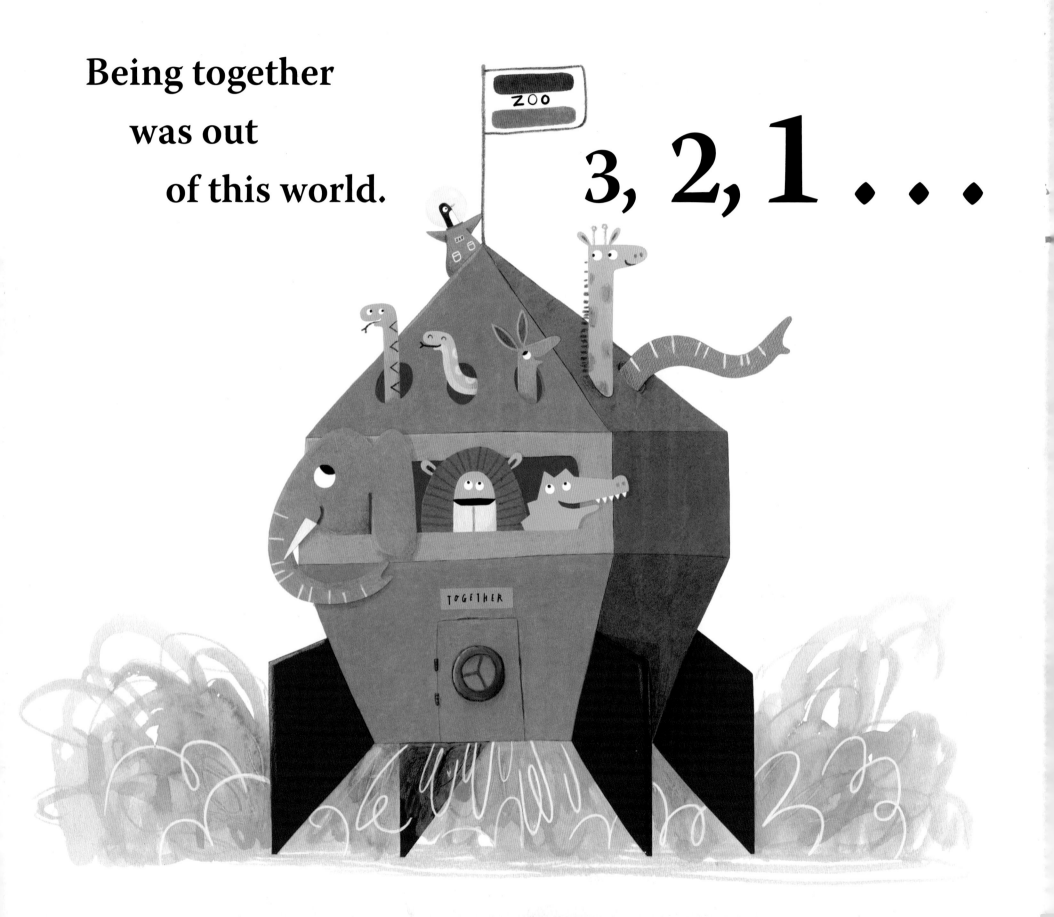